"HELP! Wild crazy girl with free spirit being held prisoner in boring middle school. Applications accepted from tall, good-looking male rescuers only." Amy giggled as she read my card aloud. "Wow, that's cute, Jo. But you aren't really going to send it are you?"

"Why not?" I asked. I attached the postcard to a red helium-filled balloon.

"But what if somebody finds it?"

"What if somebody does?"

Jenny Eastwold's

JUST CALL ME

by Victoria Althoff

To David L. and Inez Morris
With love and thanks for
truth, beauty, love,
and poetry

Cover photo by John Strange

Published by Willowisp Press, Inc.
401 E. Wilson Bridge Road, Worthington, Ohio 43085

Printed in the United States of America

10 9 8 7 6 5 4 3 2 1

ISBN 0-87406-289-6

One

"**O**UCH!" I yanked the elastic band out of my hair in one tug. With it I pulled several long strands of dark brown hair.

Amy Pollack's big blue eyes widened as we looked at ourselves in the restroom mirror. "Why'd you do that, Jo?" Amy asked. "I think your ponytail looks great now that your hair's getting long."

"Yeah, well, I'm tired of it," I said, and watched my mouth turn down. I bent my knees so that I could see the top of my head and began brushing my hair out. I didn't want to tell her what Jim Santo had said. She'd just laugh and tell me to ignore him anyway.

"Let's hurry," Amy said. "I don't want to miss the balloon launch."

"You go ahead," I suggested. "I'll catch up."

"No, I'll wait," Amy said. She cocked her head, making her blond curls bounce. "Is there

5

anything wrong, Jo?" she asked.

"Everything's just great. Why?" I asked, putting my brush into my purse. My mind was on Jim Santo. He's been my neighbor since we were little kids. We used to play in a sandbox together. Well, this morning he remembered my nickname. When I was little I wore pigtails, and everybody called me *Tails*.

"If everything's so super, then why are you so grouchy?" Amy asked. "It's Spirit Week, remember? You were the one who talked the student council and the faculty into having it. So, cheer up!"

"Okay," I said as I finished washing my hands. "I'm coming."

It isn't that Jim is anybody I care about. But he would have to drag up that old nickname. I had just walked into geography class. Jim stood up across the room and yelled, "Hey, Tails! Now you're a tall tail!" We were studying tall tales in English that week. He thought he was being really funny, and so did everybody else. The entire class burst out laughing, even Mr. Reynolds. I just stood there feeling my face turn red and trying to smile. You'd think I'd get used to that sort of thing. Instead, I vowed never to wear a ponytail again.

Amy and I walked side by side down the hallway of Medbrook Middle School. I wasn't trying to keep anything from Amy. She's my best friend. But I didn't think she'd understand. Amy is tiny, with a perky turned-up nose, dazzling curls, and all her body parts in exactly the right proportions. She doesn't date, but already boys crowd around her at parties. And we're only thirteen. I still don't know why she likes me, the incredible hulk of the whole school.

When I was ten, I grew really fast. I was suddenly a head taller than anyone else in my class. And nobody's caught up yet. If I hear one more joke about how the weather is up here, I think I'll scream. Jim Santo is the next tallest kid in the class, and I look down on the part in his hair. How could petite little Amy appreciate that kind of life?

"Are you moping over what Jim Santo said to you in geography class today?" Amy asked as I opened the front door.

I gulped and let go of the door. It banged heavily against my foot. "Ow!" I cried. I had a sudden vision of myself with flat toes for the rest of my life. I figured that if Amy knew what happened in geography when she wasn't in the class, then the whole school must know. "Amy, how do you always know what's bothering me?"

"You're my friend," she said simply. "I'm

sorry Jim upset you. But you usually laugh about your height, Jo. People don't realize it bothers you to be five foot eight."

"And five-eighths," I put in.

Amy chuckled. "That's just what I mean. You always make jokes about your height. Nobody knows that the teasing upsets you. Everybody really likes you, Jo, including Jim Santo."

"Right," I said, and shoved the door open again. "Look out, Medbrook, here come the fairy princess and the jolly green giant."

"Quit it, Jo." I could hear the irritation in her voice.

"All right, I'm not green," I corrected myself.

The front lawn of the school looked like a gigantic painting with bright reds, blues, pinks, and yellows on a dark green canvas. I put my glasses on, and the canvas became grass. The bright splashes took on the shapes of people and balloons.

A bunch of the kids were lined up at tables writing on postcards. Others were waiting to attach their postcards to balloons. There were several teachers filling balloons with helium and helping kids tie strings and cards to the balloons. Here and there a balloon escaped and swung upward. Over by the pine trees,

Rudy Foster was busily attaching his card to a cluster of six bright red balloons.

"C'mon," Amy said. "Let's get ours ready. If nothing else will cheer you up, think about how we're missing algebra today because of the balloon launch."

"That's true," I agreed. I followed her down the steps and over to the nearest table.

Mrs. Keller handed Amy a stamped postcard. Then she smiled up at me. "Oh, there you are, Jo. I've been looking for you." She gave me that look she's always giving me, and I knew what was coming. "Jo, we're about to run out of balloons. Would you go get the extra box for me? It's on the top shelf of my closet." She fished in her dress pocket and handed me a key. "Here you go," she said.

Amy looked at me as if she knew the request bugged me. "I'll do it, Mrs. Keller," she said quickly.

"No, Amy, I'm afraid I need Jo. She can reach the top shelf. I don't want anyone to have to stand on a chair," Mrs. Keller said.

I took the key and went inside to Mrs. Keller's room. It's always that way. At home, at school, the only thing I'm good for is to reach the high shelves. The only people who might ever want to marry me are either basketball stars or people who need me to

9

reach things. I hate basketball! I grabbed the balloons and went out again.

Jim Santo was standing near the table when I brought Mrs. Keller her balloons. "Aw, you lost your tail," he said, mocking sadness.

"Go away, little boy," I said. Jim just grinned and walked away humming "High as a Mountain." It was a song we sang in choir.

Amy was still there waiting for me. I turned to her and said, "I could—"

"Never mind," Amy interrupted. "He's not worth it. Here, fill out your postcard."

"What do you put on this?" I asked her.

"Whatever you want, I guess. I just said we were having spirit week at school and asked the finder to please return the card. Then I put my name and address on the stamped side."

"Okay," I said, and took the pen she handed to me. I stared at the card for a minute and then had an idea. When I finished writing, I handed the postcard to Amy.

"HELP! Wild, crazy girl with free spirit being held prisoner in boring middle school. Applications accepted from tall, good-looking male rescuers only." Amy giggled as she read my card aloud. "Wow, that's cute, Jo. But you aren't really going to send it, are you?"

"Why not?" I asked. I attached the postcard

to a red helium-filled balloon.

"But what if somebody finds it?"

"What if somebody does?" I said. "Amy, nobody ever reads these things. They'll just return it, if they do." Amy covered her mouth with her hands.

"Everybody ready?" Mr. Merwin shouted through a portable microphone. "Now on the count of three, let your balloons go." The schoolyard quieted a little. The excited talking around us settled to a few giggles. For a moment I could hear the breeze riffling the tree leaves. Then Mr. Merwin shouted, "One, two, THREE!"

Kids yelled and cheered. The balloons lifted like a huge rainbow cloud and rose slowly into the sky, spreading into clumps of two or three, then drifting apart.

"There they go," I said. We watched mine go up with Amy's. The two balloons floated together for a while. Then mine picked up speed and swung away in the wind. It sailed over the top of the school and out of sight.

"Well, I hope you won't be sorry." Amy sounded a little worried. "But what if somebody comes looking for a wild, crazy girl?"

"Then I'll lie," I said with a smile.

Two

"WHAT'S up, Tails?" Jim leaned against the locker next to mine and grinned at me. "Heard from your balloon yet? It's been a week, you know."

"No, I haven't. And will you quit calling me that name? Or is your mind like concrete—permanently set?" I swung the locker door back hard. But he jumped, and I missed him.

"You're too slow, Jo." He laughed. "I haven't heard from mine, either. Jennifer More got her card back from Springfield, though. By the way, did you get your class pictures yesterday?"

I shuddered. "Don't mention them. I must have had the flu when they took them. I look really pale, like Dracula had just drained my blood."

"Mine were pretty bad, too," he said. "But trade me anyway. We can use each other's for dart board practice." He held out his picture to me.

"That's not a bad idea." I handed him one of mine. "Maybe it'll improve my aim."

I looked at his picture. Actually, it made him look pretty good. Jim didn't have his usual wide grin, just a pleasant smile. His wildly curly brown hair was tamed into neat curves, and his blue eyes really showed up behind his glasses. I looked from the picture to Jim. He isn't much shorter than I am. I hadn't realized how much older he looked lately. Of course I wasn't going to tell him that. "Wow, Jim. I'll be sure to not let my dog see this. She has a weak stomach."

"Yeah, I was just thinking of putting your picture on the door to keep out the mice," he said as the bell rang for class. "See you, Jo." I watched him walk away. We were both going to algebra, but I guessed he didn't want to wait for me.

* * * * *

I didn't get to tell Amy about Jim until we were walking home and comparing pictures that afternoon. Amy's, of course, was gorgeous. She could wear a potato sack, and still that golden hair would glisten, and her blue eyes would sparkle.

"It doesn't surprise me that Jim wanted your picture," Amy said matter-of-factly. "I told you he likes you."

I handed Amy a picture. She looked at it critically.

"This isn't bad, Jo. You could use a little makeup, that's all," Amy said, and then changed the subject. "Did you hear that Rudy Foster's balloon card came back from West Virginia? That's the farthest yet."

"As many balloons as Rudy had tied to it, it should have gone to the next planet instead of the next state," I said. "And by the way, I haven't heard anything from mine. See, you worried for nothing."

When we got to my house, we dumped our books on a chair and headed for the kitchen. Mom had left a note saying she was working late and that I should fix supper for Dad. Beside her note was a letter addressed to me.

I looked at the strange handwriting and then at the postmark. It was from somebody here in town. Suddenly I felt my hands go cold.

"Well, aren't you going to open it?" Amy demanded over my shoulder. I looked at her, and she blushed. "I'm sorry. It's none of my business, is it? I'm just really curious who it is. If it's your balloon answer . . ." She didn't finish, but stared expectantly.

I looked at the letter. "I can't, Amy. You open it!"

She took it, licked her lower lip, and then turned the letter over. "There's a return address," she said. "Rod Lingst, Newberry Street. He lives on the other side of town." She smiled mischievously. "What kind of guy has a name like Rod?"

"The guy who started *Twilight Zone*, for one," I answered.

Amy frowned.

"Oh, go on! Open it, Amy!"

Amy was taking her time getting her fingernails under the envelope flap. I tried to grab the letter, but she turned away. "Sit down, you wild, crazy female, and let's see what we have here." She pulled out a sheet of paper. "Darling! Where have you been all my life! I've been waiting for someone wild, someone looking for fun, someone with a free spirit—"Amy looked up.

"Did he really say that?" I asked.

"No, I didn't read it." Amy grinned. "I don't read other people's mail. Here, you read it. I'll get us some milk."

I looked at the paper.

Dear Mysterious Jo,

I'm sorry that I shot down your balloon while I was target practicing. I know all about boring middle schools since I went to one myself just last year. You didn't send along an application form, so I supplied my own. After I filled it out, it seemed like a good idea to send you one, too.

Naturally, I need to have some information about you and your captivity so that I can plan the rescue. Therefore, I've included some of my own questions.

> *Rod Lingst*
> *Damsel Rescuers Limited*

I looked in the envelope. There was another paper that was typed to look like a job application form. It had a picture attached to the bottom—a snapshot of Rod in cutoffs standing beside a lake. He was gorgeous! He had dark, wavy hair and wide-set, dark eyes. And he had a broad, mischievous smile. He looked like he might just wink at any minute.

"Amy! Come see this!" I practically yelled. Already, I was glancing down the application page.

16

Amy set the glasses of milk on the table and picked up the letter.

"Look at this, Amy, I can't believe it. He's five foot ten, taller than I am. Brown hair, brown eyes—" I was reading out loud, and my face couldn't stop grinning. "He likes animals and music and rescuing fair damsels. He goes to West!" I looked up.

Amy was laughing. "He sounds pretty interesting," she said, and took the application paper I handed her. "Did you see his questions for you?"

That's when I stopped grinning. "No, where?" I asked, and I felt a little chill.

"Here at the bottom," Amy said, pointing. " 'How old are you? How tall?' He has blanks for hair, eyes, interests . . . ."

"Oh, I'd forgotten about that," I said. I gulped my milk and went up to my room. Amy followed.

My room is the whole second floor. Our house was built in the 1920s, and the second floor has a low-pitched ceiling with windows all around that let in a lot of light. Dad put in a tiny bathroom with a shower for me, and Mom and I put up blue flowered wallpaper.

Amy sprawled across the blue and white quilt on the antique bed Grandma had given me and stared at the letter.

17

"So, are you going to send him your picture?" she wanted to know.

"No way," I said.

"Why not? I sure would."

"If I looked like you, I would, too," I told her. "But I feel like King Kong." I hunted for a pair of tennis shoes. The ones I'd been wearing suddenly felt tight.

"That's silly, Jo," Amy said. "I wish you'd quit putting yourself down because you're tall. Lots of people are tall—fashion models, for instance."

"Right, but they have figures to match," I said as I yanked on a pair of jeans. "In case you haven't noticed, I look more like a football player than a fashion model."

Amy laughed. "Hardly, Jo." She rolled off the bed, and stood with her hands on her hips. Then she looked at me critically. "Well, your figure isn't developed yet. But you could try some makeup. I'll help you. Then you could send him your picture. Honestly, you don't need to lose weight."

"Well, I could sure stand to reorganize it a bit, then," I said as I stuffed my feet into a pair of running shoes that were as tight as the tennis shoes. "I'll try some makeup—if you'll help."

Amy smiled. "Of course I'll help, Jo. We'll

make you look so great that Rod Lingst won't stand a chance." She frowned at Rod's letter that was still lying on the bed. "But what will really win him over is the letter you're going to write. That's your specialty, Jo. You'll be so clever that he won't be able to resist you."

I smiled, but I was sure that Amy didn't know what she was talking about.

Three

AFTER school the next day, I put a casserole in the oven for my mother and took off for a while. When I don't know what to do, I go off and walk along the bike trail through the park near our house. Pretty soon I'm running, just because it feels so good to run. When the wind is blowing in my hair and my legs and arms are working, I feel like I could fly. There's just me—and the trees. And the trees are so much bigger than I am, that I don't feel like a giant.

Today I just wanted to think. I figured I could probably get back before my dad got home from work. My dad is the head of computer programming for an insurance company. I get my height from my dad. I just hope I don't grow to be as tall as he is. My mother is shorter. She's a research chemist. When she's working on a project she's sometimes late every night for weeks. Even during busy times, though, she usually tries to come home for dinner and then go back to work later.

The bike trail is paved through the park. Everything around the trail was pretty muddy from last week's rains. I slogged along through the wet part where water still covered the trail. Then as the pavement dried, I picked up some speed.

I kept wondering what I was going to do about that letter from Rod Lingst. Amy was really excited about it. But Amy's a romantic. She has all kinds of ideas and plans for us. I just kept reminding myself that this whole thing was a joke from the start. That was the fun part about the letter. Rod talked about rescuing me from a boring middle school. Now if I could just figure out what to write back.

The sky was pretty dark when I left the woods. I started pounding for home, hoping the casserole wasn't burned yet. Car lights appeared behind me, and I moved away from the road. But the car slowed down and stayed behind me. I ran faster, and the car still followed. I heard a window rolling down, and then somebody called. "Jo? Jo Hartrum? Wait a minute, will you?" I stopped and turned around. The car stopped, too. A tall woman with short straight hair got out. It was

Ms. Okes, the physical education teacher at school.

"I thought that was you, Jo," she said. "I didn't know you were a runner."

I shrugged my shoulders. "I'm not. Really."

"Well, you look pretty good to me." She put her thumbs through the belt loops of her jeans and cocked her head to look down at me. Ms. Okes is the only woman teacher who's taller than I am. "Why don't you come out for track?"

A picture ran through my mind of all those little kids lining up at the starting line with me towering over them. And I hate to wear gym clothes, I thought. They just show off how big I am. I tried to find an excuse. "No, uh—I—I'm just late for dinner, Ms. Okes. I don't really—"

"You come and see me in the morning, Jo. I want to talk with you. Okay?" She smiled and got back into her car. "I'd give you a ride, but the practice will do you more good," she said as she drove off.

I hurried toward home. By the time I got there, the casserole was already out cooling on the counter, and Dad was sitting there waiting for me.

"Hi, Jo! I rescued the casserole. How's it going?" Dad grinned. His curly, brown hair was hanging over his forehead.

"Uh, fine, Dad. I want to take a quick shower, okay?"

"Sure. Your mother just called to say she's on her way. I'll make a salad."

"Great!" I started upstairs.

"Then you can tell me who Rod Lingst is," he said.

I nearly fell up the steps.

My dad is a terrific guy. While I showered, I thought about how understanding he is and how much fun he is to talk with. Then I tried to figure out what I was going to tell him. The truth, of course. Well, almost, anyway. But I didn't know how he'd react if I gave him the full details of my postcard.

When I got dressed and went downstairs, my mother was just coming in the door. She didn't even bother to change out of her suit. She looked tired, and her hair was all falling down. Mom has thick, shiny brown hair. On weekends, she wears it down and curled around her face. But at work, it's pulled up in a tight bun. Often, she wears a cap as well, to keep her hair away from the chemicals.

"Supper looks good," Mom said as she sat down. "Thanks a lot, Jim."

"Rough day?" he asked. He put the salad on the table, then leaned over and kissed her.

Mom nodded. "I am so tired tonight, but I did get finished."

"The plastics project? Good for you, Jane!"

"Tomorrow I can write up the results. I'm going to recommend some further research in a couple of directions."

"Who knows?" My dad pushed his glasses up on his nose and said, "One of these days we'll have everything from lawn furniture to surgical implements made with PolyHartrum."

Mom laughed. "Don't hold your breath. These days they name discoveries for the guy who puts up the research money."

Dad spread his hands. "Oh well, so much for fame in the field of chemistry," he said. "Oh, by the way, Jo, did you get that letter? Who is Rod Lingst, anyway?"

I wasn't ready for the question yet. I know my face turned red. Mom sat up straighter and looked at me. I said, "Uh—nobody, really." Then I stammered some more before I caught my breath and said, "He found my postcard— you know, from the balloons we sent up at school."

"Hey! That's great!" Dad said. "Did he say where he found it?"

"Yeah. It only went to the other side of town," I answered. "Rod goes to West. He said he shot my balloon down while he was doing some target practice."

Mom frowned. "He was shooting a gun?"

"No, arrows. He's on the archery team. Anyway, my balloon landed too close to be interesting. Rudy Foster's card went to West Virginia. Of course he tied about a dozen balloons to it." I hoped I could change the subject away from Rod Lingst. I didn't know what my parents would think if they knew what I'd written on the postcard.

After dinner, when I'd finished my homework, I looked at Rod's letter and application again. What on earth was I going to say to him? I got out some stationery and wrote, *"Dear Rod."* Then I stared at it for a while. Finally, I called Amy and asked her to come over.

* * * * *

"Boy, was I glad when you called," Amy said when I let her in. We went upstairs, and she flopped on my bed dramatically. "The twins were incredible tonight." Amy has a pair of younger twin brothers. Most people can't tell them apart. Not only do they look alike, but they're both about as ornery as seven-year-olds can be.

"What were they up to?" I asked her.

"They put books and stuff under the hall rug to prop it up into hills and valleys, and they were driving all their cars and trucks over it."

"What's so bad about that?"

"*Vroom! Vroom!*" She mimicked loud motor noises. "You can't hear anything over there, that's what." She sat up suddenly as if she just remembered something. "Have you written to Rod yet?"

I was sitting at my desk, so I picked up the empty sheet of paper and showed it to her.

"Jo!" Amy frowned in exasperation. "What's so hard? Just tell him—tell him about school. Tell him about how you got the idea for Spirit Week and convinced the student council and the faculty that it was a good idea. Tell him—what's the matter?"

"I'm too dull for somebody like this," I said, looking at Rod's photo.

"No, you're not. Look, Jo, if you don't want to write, then just call him." She came over and picked up the phone and dialed information. "I'd like the number for the Lingst residence on Newberry."

My heart pounded as we listened to the computer voice give the number. Amy wrote the number on the envelope.

"Oh, Amy, I can't," I wailed. "I wouldn't know what to say."

Amy shook her head and put down the phone. Then she picked up the application. "What does he ask, anyway? Age?"

"I'm too old for this nonsense," I said disgustedly.

"No." Amy got an impish grin on her face. "Actually, you're exactly old enough." She wrote on the application. "Now, height?"

"Same as Godzilla," I said.

Amy gave me her disgusted look. "Try again."

"Feet reach the ground?" I asked.

She smiled. "Exactly. That's great," she said, writing the answer on the form. "Eyes?"

"Two." I grinned.

"Hair?"

"Yes. Okay?"

"That's more like it, Jo. You're the funniest person I know, so let this guy know it, too."

I pulled out my stationery and started to write.

> *Prisoners at Medbrook Middle School are generally kept chained to the cafeteria wall where they are force-fed leftovers from the thirteenth century. It's a terrible fate. When you've worked out the details of your rescue plan, just call me.*

Four

THAT night, I woke up around two A.M. feeling nervous. The moonlight streaming through my window made the furniture look like dark ghosts. Among the bumps and bulges of stuff on top of my desk, the moon picked up the squarish shape of the envelope. Amy and I had completed the crazy letter to Rod and had given all his application questions silly answers. Then Amy had put one of my awful school pictures in with the letter.

"Don't!" I'd said. "Those are the worst pictures I ever had."

"No, they aren't," Amy had answered, and sealed the envelope.

"You mean I've had worse?" I'd asked.

Amy had given me a look of disgust. "No, I mean you look just fine in the picture. Rod will think so, too," she'd said.

Now I was lying in bed thinking about

sending him that awful picture. "It's not important," I told myself. "It's just a joke, anyway." I lay there for a little while watching the moonlight on the envelope. "Well, if it *is* just a joke . . ." I muttered to myself. Then I got up and rummaged in the desk drawer in the dark until I found another envelope. I tore open the letter, and my picture fell out onto the desk. I stuffed the letter into the new envelope. Before I sealed it, I turned on the light. Amy's new picture smiled up at me from the desk. I picked up her picture and stuck it into the envelope. I licked the flap and sealed the letter. Then I turned off the light and went back to bed.

* * * * *

"I'm glad you came, Jo," Ms. Okes said when I showed up at her office just before lunchtime the next day.

I wondered if I had a choice not to come, but I didn't say anything.

"Don't look so glum," she told me. "All I want you to do is warm up a little, run around the track once, and let me time you."

"Ms. Okes, I don't—"

"Please try, Jo," she said before I had a chance to object.

So I started walking around the track. Soon I was jogging. Then I began to notice things. The white line flowed out in front of me on the track like a tiny river. The sound of the wind echoed in my ears. My arms and legs felt like they were floating through space—

"Okay, Jo." Ms. Okes stopped me. She was shaking her head a little and smiling, more to herself than to me. "Go shower and get to class. Can you come by after school today?"

What could I say? How could I tell her I didn't want to be on the track team? I hadn't planned to really run the way I do at the park. It just sort of happened. I forgot what I was doing. I had no idea what my time was, but already I knew what Ms. Okes was going to say to me. Even if I'd been lousy, she'd look at my long legs and figure she could make something of me. Well, no matter what she thought, I didn't want to go out and make a spectacle of myself.

I'd missed lunch, and running had made me hungry. But I was already late. I had to hurry to get to algebra class before the late bell.

In class, Mr. Bosworth gave us an assignment to work on, and then he left. The room was quiet until I got hiccups. The hiccups got noisier and noisier, and I didn't know what to do. Mr. Bosworth never let anyone out of class for any reason. Did I dare go get some water? I held my breath, but it didn't work. I looked over at Amy. She was grinning. The hiccups were getting really loud. All the kids around me were giggling.

Finally, somebody tapped me on the shoulder. I looked around. From the next aisle, Jim Santo handed me a roll of candy. I helped myself to a piece and handed him back the pack. It really helped. As soon as I started sucking on the candy, the hiccups stopped. Sometimes Jim can be really nice, I thought.

After class I went over to thank him. "Hey, Tails!" he said. "Why didn't you eat some lunch? Are you on a diet or something? Or are you trying to impress a guy?"

"I had other things to do," I said. "Besides, how'd you know I didn't eat lunch?"

He shook his head. "You always sit in the same place—like a permanent fixture in the middle of that bunch of girls. I thought you held the table up. I was surprised it didn't fall over today. Where were you, anyway?"

"Checking the weather," I said. "If it snows, I'm the first to know."

He smiled. The room had emptied, and it was getting late. He held out the roll of candy. "Here, just in case you get another quiet class. By the way, Knock-knock."

"Who's there?"

"Hiccup."

I didn't go on with it. "Do me a favor, Jim. Let's talk after your brain transplant." I hurried out of the room before he had a chance to complete the joke.

The trouble with Jim Santo, I thought as I practically ran down the hall to English class, is that he can't do or say anything nice without making a joke out of it. Particularly, he can't say anything nice to me.

Amy met me at my locker after school. "I haven't seen you all day," she said. "Did you mail the letter?"

I nodded. I didn't have the nerve to tell her I'd sent her picture, not mine. I hoped she wouldn't ask me anything more about it.

"Are you ready to go?" she asked as I gathered my books.

"Uh, no. I have to see Ms. Okes."

Amy made a face. "The gym teacher? After school? Why?"

I shrugged. "I'll tell you later when I find out myself."

Amy looked puzzled, but all she said was, "Should I wait for you?"

"No, don't bother. It could be late," I said, and slammed my locker.

As I clattered down the stairs to the gym

office, I thought about how much trouble track could be. For all I knew Ms. Okes could keep me running around her track until five o'clock. And if she did make me run again, I wasn't sure I wanted Amy watching—even if she is my best friend. I knocked on the door to Ms. Okes' office, and it opened.

"How can I talk you into joining the track team, Jo?" Ms. Okes didn't even bother to say hello.

"Ms. Okes, I don't want to," I said.

"Sit down, please." She indicated a chair across from her desk. I sat down and watched her clasp and unclasp her long-fingered hands, waiting for me to say something.

"Jo, you ran a better time than anyone on the team."

"I don't care," I said stubbornly.

"With you on the team those kids might have a better chance to win some meets. We need more good runners. In relays, you could give the team that boost they need."

"I'm sorry, Ms. Okes, but no. Please." I pleaded with her.

"If you don't want to help the school, Jo, what about yourself?"

"No!" I said. I didn't know how long I could listen to her without telling her the real reason.

"Are you too shy to run in front of people?" Ms. Okes guessed.

"No—yes—Ms. Okes, I'm already the tallest kid in the whole school. I just can't—" I wasn't sure I was making much sense.

But Ms. Okes smiled and nodded. "I understand what you mean. It's not easy to be taller than everyone around you right now." She sat back in her chair. "But being tall gives you advantages, Jo. And by the time you're a few years older, many people will be taller than you are. You can't make yourself shrink, you know."

"I know," I echoed, feeling miserable.

"What you can do, is be happy with yourself the way you are. And you can use your height instead of trying to hide it. Do me a favor."

"What?" I asked, feeling suspicious.

"Try practicing with the team for two weeks. If you hate it, then I won't say anything more. I really think you'll like it, Jo. The kids are great. I promise you won't feel out of place for more than five minutes."

"I don't know," I started. But she overruled me.

"Look, Jo. If you think you're big and clumsy, practicing running will make you more graceful. It will tone up your body and show you talents you didn't know you had. Besides, it isn't just your long legs that make you good. You're a natural runner."

I ran out of arguments and agreed to give it a try.

For the next two weeks, I practiced with the girls' track team every day after school.

They were good. Gretchen Lansdown and Jill Southwick were really nice. They helped me learn relays. And Ms. Okes was right. It was fun. Amy even thought it was a good idea for me to try the team. I was surprised how excited she was about it. She said she missed walking home with me, so we made up for it by studying together or talking on the phone every night after practice.

That's why when Mom called me to the phone one night, I expected Amy. Instead, a very deep baritone voice said, "Jo? This is Rod. Rod Lingst."

Five

"HI!" I said. All the time I was thinking, Oh, no! What do I do now?

"I decided there might be a more efficient way to communicate than by balloon," Rod said. "So I thought I'd try the phone."

His voice sounded wonderful—like a movie star or something.

"Your description was so interesting," he went on. "I mean, 'feet that reach the ground, two eyes, hair'—what more could a guy ask for?"

I giggled. So far, I hadn't been able to think of a single witty, clever, or fun thing to say. I wasn't exactly panicked—more like terrified.

"And your picture!" he went on. "Is it a recent one? I mean, do you really look like that?"

I gulped. My stomach tied itself up like the telephone cord. "It's recent, all right, but—

uh—well . . . ." I didn't know what to say. I just couldn't admit I'd sent him someone else's picture. The silence over the phone grew longer and longer while he waited for me to finish. "Uh, well, it's kind of flattering," I said. "I don't really look like that. I wear glasses."

"Oh, well. It can't be too far off, right?" Rod chuckled. "Anyway, I wanted you to know that I'm gathering my forces to mount a rescue operation to save you from dying of boredom at your school."

"On horses? With buglers bugling and guns blazing?" I asked. I decided not to think about the picture right now.

"No, that would be too obvious," he said. "Besides, the horse is off that night and the bugler is out to pasture. Or is it the other way around?"

I was laughing now. He had the greatest voice. And he was really funny. "Oh, that's all right," I said. "Mr. Merwin probably wouldn't appreciate horseshoe prints on the front lawn, anyway. He almost has a heart attack when *we* walk on it."

"My stepdad is like that sometimes. One of my friends just learned to drive, and every time he pulls into the driveway, Dad goes out to check the grass."

Just like that we moved on to talking about

our families and friends. Pretty soon I learned that Rod's stepdad was with the city planning department, and his mother sold real estate.

When I asked him if he had any brothers or sisters, he said, "I'm surrounded by females."

"Girls aren't so bad," I said. "I can tell you from firsthand experience."

"I have a little experience myself," he said. "My father died when I was eight. That left Mom and Sarah and me. But when Mom married George, I got another sister who's twelve now, and one who's six. Are you counting, Jo? That's three sisters. Then last year, Mom had a baby, and guess what?"

I was already giggling at him.

"There it is, folks." Rod sounded like a radio announcer. "The latest addition to the family is Ann. Listen, Jo. You think you have troubles being chained to the wall of the cafeteria? That's a piece of cake compared to trying to use the telephone when you have a houseful of sisters."

"I guess you have a point there."

Rod told me he'd lived on Newberry Street since he was two. We talked about movies we'd seen and songs we liked.

Then Rod said, "You know we really ought to have a spy mission to check out the lay of the land around Medbrook—so our forces will know what to expect when they get there."

"How many forces do you have?" I asked him.

"Two. What about a meeting? I know a great pizza shop near you—Antonio's. It's located on Wheeling Avenue, just south of Broadway."

"I know the place," I said. "We go there a lot."

"We could meet there and plan our strategy," he suggested. "How about two o'clock on Saturday? Can you get unchained from the wall?"

"Sure," I said. "Saturdays I can bribe the guard."

"Great! I'll see you then, Jo."

"Okay."

"Bye, Jo."

When we hung up the phone, I was grinning. It was like a real date! I was going to get to meet Rod! He sounded so nice! I loved the way he said my name. And he was funny. He had a great sense of humor. And we liked the same movies, the same kinds of music, and . . . .

I got up and whirled around my bedroom, unable to stop smiling. Then in mid-twirl, I caught sight of myself in the mirror, and remembered. "Rod thinks I look like Amy!" I sat down hard on the floor, and suddenly wanted to cry. I looked at the clock. Rod and I had been talking for almost an hour.

It's too late to call Amy tonight, I told myself. I'll talk to her in the morning. But when I tried to think of what I was going to tell her, I felt sick to my stomach. "Amy's my best friend in the world. She'll understand. She'll think it's a good joke," I said out loud. But it didn't seem funny anymore.

While I was sitting there on the floor, my mom's head appeared over the banister at the top of the stairs. "Who was that on the phone, Jo?"

"Oh, um . . ." I could feel my face getting red. "You remember the guy who found my balloon? I, uh—wrote to thank him, and he was just calling to say hi."

Mom came upstairs and sat down on my rocker. "What's he like?" she asked.

"He's funny. He makes me laugh."

"Well, are you going to get to meet him sometime?"

"We sort of set up a meeting at Antonio's on Saturday," I said. I was half-afraid she'd tell me I couldn't go and half-afraid she'd tell me I could.

"That sounds like fun," she said. "You might want to take a friend with you for this first meeting—Amy or somebody."

I got up and hugged her. "Mom, that's a

great idea," I said. Behind her, I saw myself in the mirror again. "Oh, Mom, what'll I wear?"

She smiled. "I'll tell you what. Why don't you go shopping? It's been a while since you had any new clothes. Maybe you could find a new outfit. I might even spring for some makeup."

"Mom, you're super," I said.

"I don't have time to go with you this week. But I'll give you my charge card if you promise not to go overboard."

"I promise, Mom. I'll ask Amy to go with me."

* * * * *

The next morning, I tried to talk with Amy on the way to school, but Jim Santo appeared at just the wrong moment and walked with us.

"Hello, you two," he said cheerfully. "Are you ready for the algebra test?"

My throat went dry. "What algebra test?" I yelled.

"Oh, I don't know, any of them." Jim winked. "There's bound to be one sooner or later."

I thought about strangling him. He knew just when to spring something like that on me. "Jim Santo!" I said. "I'll get you for that someday."

I hoped I'd get a chance to talk with Amy at lunch, but I'd forgotten that we had an extra track practice because of the meet on Friday. Ms. Okes had us practicing at lunch and after school. Today, she had me practicing the 440 and the relay. She told me to think of stretching out to reach farther with each stride. I tried thinking about Rod waiting for me at the end of the track. I don't know if it helped or if I was just getting better because of all the practice. What I do know is that Coach Okes' workouts really wore me out.

I didn't get to talk with Amy until after supper, and by then I didn't have nerve enough to tell her I'd sent her picture to Rod. But I asked her to go shopping and to go with me to meet Rod.

"You know I'll go shopping anytime, Jo. But why do you want me along on Saturday?" Amy asked. "You're the one who sent out an advertisement."

"But I'll be too nervous meeting him all by myself. I won't know what to say. Besides, he's bringing his friend Tim, because Tim is old enough to drive. That's how Rod's getting here. Come on, please, Amy?"

"Oh, okay. I'll come," she said.

"Thanks, Amy. By the way . . ."

"Jo, I have to go. Todd's standing here with

soap all over him, screaming. See you later."
She hung up before I got a chance to tell her
about the picture. But at least she'd promised
to come with me. Maybe I wouldn't have to
say anything. Maybe when we got there, Rod
would take one look at Amy and decide he
liked me better anyway.

I stood up, looked in the mirror, and shook
my head. No, Jo, I told myself. Even you don't
believe that one.

Six

AFTER my algebra class on Wednesday, Mr. Bosworth asked me to stay for a minute. When everyone was gone, he said, "Jo, I didn't get a paper from you on Tuesday. Did you overlook it?"

I'd forgotten all about that assignment. It was due the day after I talked to Rod. I shook my head, and felt my face turn red.

"It's not like you to miss assignments, Jo," he said. "Is anything wrong?"

"No, Mr. Bosworth. I've been working hard on the track team and getting home late. I just didn't have time," I said. "Can I make it up?"

"I'm afraid that wouldn't be fair to the rest of the class members who got their papers in on time. I'll offer an extra-credit assignment later this month. Perhaps you could do that to help make up for this."

He waited for a minute, but I didn't have

anything to say. So he just said, "Better get to your next class."

I had to run to make it on time. I felt bad that I'd forgotten Mr. Bosworth's assignment. But it didn't seem fair for him to get on me about it. There are lots of other kids who don't turn in their assignments. This was the first one I'd ever missed. I didn't want to tell him that I was so busy talking with a guy that I'd forgotten to do it. I thought that if he knew I was working on the track team, maybe he'd go a little easier on me. Well, I didn't plan to miss any other assignments, anyway.

Our team was really working hard. My relay was with Jill Southwick, Gretchen Lansdown, and Lynn Herrell. We were working pretty well together, I thought. But Coach Okes kept making us try harder to shave a second or so off our time. With me doing the last lap, there was a lot of pressure. Everybody depended on me to make up the time if we were behind.

"Stretch those legs," Coach Okes yelled at me. But it seemed like I couldn't stretch them any farther.

At first, I thought it wasn't fair of Coach Okes to put all that pressure on me when I'd just joined the team. After all, I'd never even seen a track meet before, let alone participated in one. But then I thought about Jill and Gretchen and Lynn. They were so nice to me. I liked them a lot. And they were really excited about the meet. They didn't seem to mind that Coach Okes was being so hard on us.

Jill came off the track with her brown hair dripping with sweat. But she was smiling, and her face seemed to glow. I couldn't let the team down if I could help it. So I kept pushing my legs out a little farther until I thought my kneecaps were going to fall off. I just hoped that if we lost, the others would still be my friends.

On Thursday night, practice was extra long because of the meet on Friday. Amy and I had planned to go shopping. But with practice running so late, Amy came over to the fence and told me to call when I got home. By the time we quit, there was almost nobody left around the school.

While I was walking home, Jim Santo came by on his bike. "Hi, Stretch," he said.

I guess he noticed the look on my face, because he stopped and took my books. "Here, you look beat." He strapped the books on the back of his bike. "I heard your coach telling you to stretch," he explained. "How long have you been on track?"

I started to answer, but then his face cracked

into a wide grin. "I mean, I thought you were *derailed* long ago. But I guess you've been *train*-ing, huh?"

"It's only your brain that derailed, Jim," I said. "But don't worry, it was such a small loss, nobody noticed."

I couldn't make him as mad as he made me. He just smiled and said, "I hope you can *engineer* a win in the track meet, Jo."

"Jim, you and your jokes make me glad to get home," I said as we got to my driveway.

"Thank you, thank you," he said, giving several mock bows to an imaginary audience. He handed me my books and got back on his bike.

"Thanks," I said, shaking my head in disbelief.

"Keep chugging, Jo," he called as he rode down the street toward his house.

"There's a letter for you," my mother said as I came inside. She was getting home on time these days, probably because she was between projects. "It's on the stand in the living room."

I raced in and grabbed it. Sure enough, it was from Rod. It was a card. On the front was a cartoon character in prisoner's clothes climbing over a wall, and inside it said, "Hope you'll soon be out and around." It was really a get-well card, but Rod had sent it as if I were a prisoner. I thought it was hilarious.

Mom walked in and saw me laughing. "What did you get?" she asked.

I had to show her. She smiled.

"Why did he send you a get-well card?" she asked.

I had to explain that I had said I was a prisoner in my school. I left out the part about being wild and crazy. She looked puzzled.

"It was a joke."

"Oh," she said, but she looked like she didn't get it.

"I have to call Amy," I said. "I hope she still wants to go shopping."

"Tell her I can drive you over to the mall after supper," Mom suggested.

It was already almost dark when Amy and I finally got to the shopping mall.

As we were walking in, I pulled out Rod's card and showed it to Amy. She was really impressed. "This guy's great, Jo. He has a sense of humor that's as good as yours."

"Yeah," I said. "He really sounds nice on the phone, too. Now if we can just find something spectacular for me to wear Saturday!"

"What are you looking for?" she asked as we walked.

I shrugged. "I don't know. Something that

will make me look short and thin and pretty—maybe even blond."

"But then he wouldn't recognize you." Amy giggled.

I bit my tongue. How little she knows, I thought. It reminded me that sometime that evening I had to tell her about the picture. It was just a joke, but I didn't know how she'd take it when I told her. I could feel my ears turning red just thinking about it.

Hunter Park Mall is not the largest in the world. We looked in every store. I stood in front of about a hundred mirrors and remembered why I hate to go shopping. There are jeans long enough for me but not much else. And the tops all have sleeves that stop way above my wrists. I felt like I was trying to get into Amy's clothes, not ones for me.

"Let's give up," I told Amy. I was standing in a dressing room in front of a mirror and looking at a pale turquoise-blue sweater that sagged in front and barely stretched past my elbows in the sleeves.

"How about a short-sleeved sweater over a blouse?" Amy suggested.

"Where are we going to find a blouse with long enough sleeves?" I asked her.

"We'll look for a short-sleeved blouse, too," Amy said decisively, and hurried out.

I had to admit that Amy did a good job picking clothes for me. We found a blue striped blouse and blue sweater that would look great with a pair of jeans I already had.

The fun part of the evening was looking for some new makeup. I sat on a stool at the counter while a saleswoman carefully applied soft aqua eye shadow, eyeliner, blush, and lipstick only a tiny bit darker than my lips.

"You don't want much makeup," the woman said as she showed me how to use the eye shadow. "Use just enough to make your features stand out, but not enough for anyone to notice you're wearing it."

The saleslady stepped back so I could see myself in the mirror. I could hardly believe it! I looked great. It was me, all right—but slightly different.

"You have such nice dark eyes," the saleswoman said. "Even the glasses don't hide them."

"I feel great!" I said, grinning, as we walked out of the mall to meet Amy's mother.

"I'm glad you got the makeup," Amy said. "It really looks nice on you."

"I hope Mom agrees."

Amy laughed. "Now you have to learn to use all that stuff the way the lady showed you."

I groaned. "You watched. You can help me."

"Don't worry, Jo. You can do it. It just takes a little practice."

It wasn't until after I was back home that I remembered I had to tell Amy I'd sent her picture to Rod. I felt bad about it, but it was too late to call her. I vowed I'd tell her first thing in the morning.

*　*　*　*　*

Amy had said it would only take a little practice to learn to use the makeup. So on Friday morning, I got up a whole hour early to try it out. But the aqua eye shadow didn't look the way it had looked in the store. Instead, it looked darker. I tried to rub some of it off and got it smeared all around my eyes.

I washed my face and tried again, but it still wasn't right. I decided to go on to the eyeliner. I had trouble holding my hand steady enough, and I kept blinking. Then I jabbed myself in the eye and had to wash my eye out with drops. The lipstick was at least in the right place. But it looked a lot darker than it had looked when the lady put it on. And the blush seemed to be too far down on my cheeks.

I stepped back to get the full effect, and saw something like a ring-eyed owl peering back at me. It was getting late. I thought about taking it all off but I had promised myself that I'd use this makeup now that I'd bought it. I put my glasses on and hoped they covered up any mistakes.

I think my mother coached my dad on what not to say. When I came into the kitchen, his eyes widened, and his mouth dropped. Then he picked up the newspaper and hid behind it. "Morning, Jo," he said, but I heard a laugh in his voice.

"Um, Jo," my mother said, "you know, you don't need as much makeup in the daytime as you do at night."

She didn't say anything I hadn't been already thinking. I knew it looked awful. I just didn't know what to do about it. All the same, it upset me when she said something about it. So I snapped at her.

"All right," I said. "I'll take it off." I ran back upstairs and scrubbed all the makeup off my face and went to school without it. I didn't even say good-bye.

"Where's the makeup?" Amy asked me when I came out.

"In the trash now," I said angrily.

"Oh, Jo," Amy was sympathetic. "I know. The first time I tried to put makeup on, my dog hid under the bed and barked at me. I'll come over on Saturday, and we can practice.

You didn't really throw it all out, did you?"

"No, but I was thinking about it," I said. And since she'd mentioned it, I was also thinking about something else that I had forgotten. The track meet was this afternoon—my first. I hoped it wouldn't be a disaster, too.

Seven

I was glad the day was bright and sunny. Our track is asphalt, so it's not too hard to run on. But it can get slippery if it's wet, and the grass can be miserable for the other events if it's muddy. I told myself there was nothing to be nervous about. Running is easy for me. And besides, it didn't matter whether I won or not. I was just doing it because Ms. Okes asked me to. If I lost, she might cut me from the team. Then I wouldn't have to worry about it anymore.

But when I got there and watched my teammates warming up, my feelings changed. I knew I really did want to win. I wanted to win for them and for Medbrook, and also for me.

Coach Okes came over to me as I was doing some stretching exercises. "Just remember all we did in practice, Jo. It won't be any different. Good luck to you."

I thought she was talking to me because I was new and this was my first meet. Then I noticed she stopped and said something to each girl.

We all sat together to watch the events we weren't involved in. Two other schools, Crestview and Foxgrove, were competing against us. Crestview had a really good team. Lynn Herrell came in second to the Crestview girl in the hurdles. Jill Southwick won a close long jump against a Foxgrove girl named Emmy. Gretchen Lansdown beat the runners from Crestview and Foxgrove in the 100-yard dash. We were all up against the fence yelling our heads off when she pulled away just before they got to the finish line.

Then it was time for the 440. As I got up, I heard somebody yell from the bleachers.

"Hey, Jo! Good luck!"

I looked over and saw Amy. Jim was next to her. He was the one who'd yelled. I also noticed somebody else. Mr. Bosworth was sitting on the bleachers all alone. I wondered if he'd come to find out whether or not I was really on the track team.

I ran over and gave my glasses to Jill to hold. Then I lined up with the girls from the other two teams. I was taller than they were, but they looked like they were in really good shape. Nobody smiled. They both looked straight out ahead of them. I did, too. Then we started. I was running in my usual way. I forgot the track and the people around me. Just the steady rhythm of my arms and the slap of my feet were all I heard. My head forgot everything else except running. It was wonderful.

But there was a flash—something white—and I realized someone was beside me. My brain was outside of myself, watching with interest, but without making any change in me. It was as if I were two people, one running, and another one watching. Finally, I realized the runner was ahead of me, and something told my feet to move. Faster. Faster. Stretching for each stride, my legs gulped the ground in front of me and threw it up behind. The world was blue and green around me, and there was only the slap of shoes and a gnawing ache growing in my body. I ignored the pain and stretched my legs. I came up beside the runner, feet pounding, seeing her in a blur.

And then the blur was gone. She was out ahead, and I knew I couldn't catch her. But I tried. My ears echoed with the sound of my feet pounding and my blood rushing through my body. I was nearer, nearer, and then suddenly it was over.

I passed her slowing down, but it was too late. The girl from Crestview, number 8, was leaning over the fence, panting hard. The girl from Foxgrove followed practically on my heels as we crossed the finish.

A whole carload of aches suddenly attacked my legs and knees, and my heart wouldn't slow down enough to let me talk. I went over to the winner. She was nearly as tall as I am, with sandy hair and clear blue eyes. I stuck out my hand and managed to say, "Congratulations."

She smiled shyly and shook my hand. "You nearly had me," she panted. "My name's Kathy."

The Foxgrove girl, Emmy, joined us as we walked off the track together. "I'm worn out," Kathy said. "It's usually easier to win, because I'm the tallest person at most meets."

"Are you in eighth grade?" Emmy asked her.

"No, seventh."

Emmy smiled. "Me, too. I guess I'll be running against you for another year, then."

I was surprised to be the oldest. "Are you the tallest person in your class?" I asked Kathy.

She wrinkled her nose. "I guess maybe I am. Everyone in my family is tall, though. I don't think much about it."

"Does everyone in your family run?" Emmy asked her.

Kathy nodded. We said good-bye and went back to our teams.

"Where's Crestview?" I asked Lynn.

"I don't know—the south end of town, maybe?"

"I think it's either east or west. It's not north," Jill put in.

When Gretchen, Jill, Lynn, and I lined up for the 440 relay, I noticed that Kathy was the anchor on the Crestview team, and Emmy was anchor on the Foxgrove team. Oh, well, I thought. I tried, didn't I?

And then we began. Everybody was yelling and waiting for the next person. Gretchen came through her lap first, and we were a fraction of a second ahead. Lynn pounded down the track. I could see her jaw set with determination. She couldn't have smiled if she tried. And then Jill was coming toward me. I stopped yelling and got ready for the baton. It seemed to take forever. The Crestview girl passed Jill. Jill gave a spurt and got to me just before the Foxgrove girl, but Kathy was already started for Crestview. Then I was running. I didn't think about anything at all now—not about Kathy, not even about winning. I just thought about running as fast and as hard as I could. I couldn't feel my legs. They moved without my knowing. I just kept stretching—moving faster and faster. There was a blur out beside me, white against the black track. And then I saw Kathy out in front again.

The next thing I knew, everyone was gathered around, congratulating us. We had come in second. Kathy Childs was the real star. I could hardly get over how good she was. Still everyone was yelling and jumping, because we'd done better than Medbrook usually does. I looked around and noticed that Gretchen looked worn out. I knew I hurt all over. Kathy and Emmy came over, and we all shook hands. When the meet was over, Coach Okes stopped by my locker.

"Nice job, Jo."

I thanked her, but she just went on as if she hadn't heard me. "We need to work on your pacing. You didn't save enough reserve for the last spurt. But it was a really good try for the first time. Congratulations."

She walked away, then came back. "You are staying on the team, aren't you?"

I nodded. She wouldn't have let me quit anyway. And I didn't want to anymore.

Jim and Amy walked home with me. They didn't say too much, except that they were glad we got second place instead of being last, the way Medbrook usually is. Jim didn't even make any of his usual wisecracks about my height. I think he knew I felt bad about not beating Kathy.

We were walking out of the parking lot when I noticed Mr. Bosworth and waved at him. Then he got into Coach Okes' car, and they drove out. I realized he hadn't come to check up on me after all. He probably carpooled with Coach Okes and was stuck for a ride.

* * * * *

When I got home, I took a long shower. Then I fell asleep, stretched across my bed. It was dark when Mom woke me up and asked if I wanted any supper. I splashed some water on my face to get the sleep out of my eyes and squinted into the mirror above the sink. My eyes reminded me that Amy was coming over the next day to help me fix my makeup. And that reminded me that we were going to meet Rod tomorrow. My shoulders tingled a little. Would he like me?

On the telephone, Rod sounded like so much fun. With a gulp, I thought about Amy. How would she take it when I told her I'd sent Rod her picture? It was all just in fun, of course. But since it was for fun, maybe I should have sent Rod a rock star's picture instead of Amy's. My stomach got a little queasy when I thought about telling Amy. But I had to tell her. The question was how. Or maybe the question was when. Time was running out. If I didn't tell her soon, she'd find out the hard way—tomorrow.

Eight

ANTONIO'S, where we were meeting Rod and his friend, has pizza, subs, soft drinks, and ice cream. The place is decorated to look like an old-time ice cream parlor. It has round, white-topped tables and black metal chairs with red and white striped seats. After school and on weekends the place is usually full of older kids. But sometimes kids my age stop there, too.

On Saturday, Amy came over just a few minutes before we had to leave for Antonio's. "I'm sorry," she said, panting as if she'd run the whole way. "I had to baby-sit, and I just got finished! Quick! Where's your makeup?"

I sat still while Amy applied the new makeup to my eyes and face. Every time I tried to tell her about the picture, she said, "Shh, don't move."

By the time Amy finished with the makeup,

we were late. We had to walk fast to get there. When Amy was in front of me, opening the door to Antonio's, I blurted, "Oh, I forgot to tell you. I sent Rod your picture instead of mine."

Amy turned around and stared at me. Her eyebrows went up, and her lips tightened. And her eyes changed from a soft blue to a hard gray. But I pushed her inside before she had a chance to say anything. She stopped in the middle of the black and white tile floor and spluttered, "Jo Hartrum, how—just how could you do such a thing? Don't you know—"

"Shh!" I said. "There he is at that table."

Rod stood up and called, "Jo! Over here!" He was very tall and every bit as good-looking as his picture. No, he was better-looking than any picture. His black hair was combed to the side, and his eyes were dark under thick brows. He was wearing a red sweater, a dark shirt, and a denim jacket. I couldn't get over how great he looked.

I gave Amy a little tug, and she came over with me. Then, very quietly she said, "I'm not playing your game, Jo. You get yourself out of this one."

I got a chill. But we sat down. "Who's your friend, Jo?" Rod asked Amy.

Before she could say anything, I spoke up.

"Amy Pollack," I said.

We ordered colas. Amy was pinching my arm while Rod introduced his friend, Tim Counts. Tim had red hair, freckles sprinkled over a round face, and a wide grin.

"Tim's a sophomore. He just got his driver's license," Rod said.

Amy perked up at the mention of a driver's license. "Was the test hard?" she asked Tim. Amy's been backing the car out of the garage for her dad practically every morning this year. She's just fourteen, but she can't wait to drive.

Tim shrugged. "I practiced a lot before I took the test. It wasn't really easy, but it wasn't awful, either."

A waitress came with our drinks and a pizza for the guys. I leaned over and whispered to Amy. "Just don't say anything, okay?"

"Only if you promise to straighten this out," Amy told me quietly.

"So, Jo, is Amy your guard?" Rod asked as he offered some pizza to Amy and me.

"Sure," I said. "I promised her a drink if—" Suddenly I realized I was answering for Jo, instead of Amy. "Uh . . . if she'd show me who the rescue forces were so I could fight them off."

Rod grinned, and his eyes sparkled. I thought he looked like he would be so nice to get to know. "A spy in our midst, huh?"

"I couldn't help it," Amy protested. "She insisted on coming along."

I added, "Und I haf valuable invormation," I said, using the voice of a German officer, straight from an old World War II movie.

"Aha, a guard who can be bought. Have some pizza," Rod said. He gestured to me, but he was staring at Amy the way most boys stare at her. "After all, she's obviously well worth rescuing."

I shook my head at the pizza. My cola tasted flat. All I wanted was for Rod to look at me the way he was looking at Amy right then.

"I'm not a bad guard," I said, although Amy was staring hard at me. "I unchain her from the wall on Saturdays, and sometimes I take her for walks on a leash."

"Yeah, she only takes me out when she needs me for something," Amy said.

She sounded so mad that I was afraid she'd give away the whole thing. I kicked her under the table.

"Ouch!" Amy cried. "Watch it, J—"

"Prisoners should be zeen und not heard," I interrupted her, but my face was getting hot. I couldn't bear for Rod to know that I was really Jo and not Amy. But Amy was mad. I didn't know how to keep her from spilling the beans.

"Maybe I should get a job as a guard," Rod said, smiling. "Then we could sneak you out on Saturdays, even if we can't manage a full-fledged escape."

"I doubt it," Amy said, glaring at me. "You don't look like the sort who would lie and cheat." I kicked her again.

"Ouch!"

"Ve must keep her under control," I said. But the whole conversation was becoming a disaster. I didn't know how to get around to explaining, and if I didn't, Amy was going to kill me.

Tim looked confused by this whole conversation. Amy asked him if he knew what we were talking about.

"I just came along for the ride," he said. "And the pizza."

"This one," Rod explained, gesturing to Amy, "put a note on a balloon, saying that she was being held prisoner and needed to be rescued."

When I saw the way Rod was enjoying Amy and the way he talked about her and to her, I felt like I'd swallowed a jar of vinegar. I didn't think things could get any worse.

And then suddenly, a pair of warm, wide hands clapped across my eyes. "Hi, Tails! Guess who?" Jim asked cheerily.

Of all the people who could have appeared in Antonio's, Jim Santo was the one most likely to give me indigestion.

"Jim, I am now convinced it's possible to communicate with aliens," I said. "I can understand you perfectly."

He ignored my remark, but let go of my eyes. "Hello, you two. Care to introduce me?"

Amy had a look on her face that plainly said she thought I deserved whatever I got from Jim. I stammered a little but managed to say, "Uh—Rod Lingst, Tim Counts, this is Jim Santo."

Both guys nodded, and Jim and Rod shook hands. I said, "I'd say something nice about you, Jim, but I'd rather tell the truth."

Amy gasped and went into a fit of coughing. I pounded her on the back.

"Do you guys go to school around here?" Jim asked.

"West High," Rod said.

"This is a private conversation," I said to Jim as Amy took a sip of her drink and tried to quit choking. "If I give you two aspirin, will you go away?"

"Take it easy, Tails. You'll poison yourself with that tongue." Jim asked Rod about West's baseball team this year, then went over to another table and sat down.

I was so relieved that he hadn't used my name I could hardly get over it. Rod asked Amy if she'd seen *Run for the Money* yet. It was supposed to be a good movie, but neither of us had seen it. I was sure he was going to ask her out, but he didn't. He just said he thought she'd like it, and we began to talk about other movies we liked.

I looked up and saw Jill and Gretchen from the track team walking into Antonio's. They waved, and Jill said, "Hi, Jo!" I don't think Rod noticed which of us she was looking at. I decided Antonio's must be the most popular place in town. If I hadn't been scared to death that somebody would call me by name, I'd have noticed what a great time the four of us were having. But I had to keep looking at the door in case someone else I knew came in.

Then Tim said, "We have to go now, Rod. I promised my mother I'd have the car back by five."

"Well, I probably should say something, then," Amy said, glaring at me.

I pleaded with her without saying a word. I just felt miserable about what she was probably going to say.

But Rod said, "I know, we haven't planned your escape. I guess we'll have to save it for next time."

"If I vill let her out," I said in my German accent, before Amy could say anything.

Tim and Rod got up, and we all walked to the door together. Rod said, "It was sure nice meeting you, Jo, and you, too, Amy."

"Uh, Rod," Amy said, as he started to walk away.

"What?" he asked, turning around to look at us.

"Right," I put in. "She said, 'Right.'" I steered Amy away.

"Why didn't you let me tell him?" Amy demanded as soon as we were out of earshot.

I knew she was mad at me, and I didn't blame her. Now that I thought about it, I felt really awful for putting her into a position like that, especially since I didn't tell her about it ahead of time.

But then she said, "If you could have straightened this mess out, you could be looking forward to seeing him again."

I realized that in spite of what I did to her, she was still thinking of me.

"There won't be any seeing him again," I said firmly. "Oh, Amy, he's so nice, I just couldn't bear for him to think the girl he's been talking to on the phone is me."

"Oh, Jo, stop that! What's the matter with you?"

"Well, when he looked at you the way he did—oh, I don't know. He really likes you, Amy. I couldn't stand for him to know *I* was Jo. He'd never look at *me* that way. Maybe you'd better change your name."

Amy sighed and put her arm around me. "Rod would like you, Jo, if you gave him a chance. How can I convince you of that?"

"Don't even try," I said. "It's too late now, anyway."

As we walked home together, I thought about what a mess I'd made of things. Rod thought Amy was terrific. I wanted him to like me instead, but it was all my fault that he didn't. And Amy had every right to never speak to me again. But she was still as loyal a friend as ever. I felt terrible.

Nine

“OKAY, everyone, that was a very good Monday practice. Remember to be here as soon as possible after classes end tomorrow to warm up.” Coach Okes looked around at us. I was just about ready to drop. Gretchen’s hair was plastered to her head, and she was panting.

We were trying to get ready for another meet on Thursday. And there was the big city-wide meet at County Stadium in three weeks. All the teams in the city would be there.

“That’s all for today,” Coach Okes said. Then she added, “Oh, Jo Hartrum. When you get showered, I want to see you.”

I never know what to expect when I knock at Coach Okes’ office. When I got there, she was working on some papers, but when she saw me, she tipped back her chair and said, “Sit down, Jo. Close the door, please.”

I sat and waited while she looked at me with an expression of curiosity. Finally she frowned and said, "I understand from Dan Bosworth that track practice keeps you from doing your algebra."

It was the last thing I expected. I didn't know what to say. In all the excitement about the track meet and about Rod, I never once thought about that missed assignment in algebra. And I sure never thought that Mr. Bosworth would talk with Ms. Okes. I stared at her for a minute, but she waited. The room was so quiet that I could hear the soft tick of the clock.

Finally, I stammered, "No, uh, it's all right, now. I can handle it. I just—"

Ms. Okes leaned forward, her arms over her desk. Her eyes were very blue and very serious. "Jo, I don't want to make it hard on you, but you know your studies are very important. Track is also important. But it's an extracurricular activity."

"I know, Ms. Okes, but—"

"That means," she went on as if I hadn't said anything, "that if you can't get your schoolwork done, not only do you lose out in your studies, but I get in trouble for taking too much of your time."

"But I didn't actually—what?"

She nodded and smiled, but she wasn't really joking. "You see, the academic teachers believe that any kind of sport must come second. Even though I believe in physical fitness, I have to agree that you must get your schoolwork done. Now, is there any way I can help you with your algebra? Do you need a tutor?"

I realized that Ms. Okes had no idea that I was a good student. "No, Ms. Okes," I said. "I'm doing all right now."

"But if you have a problem, please let me help you, Jo."

She wasn't going to let it go. I realized I had to tell her the truth. "I'm sorry, Ms. Okes," I said. I know my face was red. I could feel it getting hot, and my throat was dry as I tried to talk. "I just forgot to do the assignment. I got a phone call that lasted a long time, and I just forgot about it. Then when Mr. Bosworth asked me . . . " I couldn't look at her face, so I stared at my hands.

"You told Mr. Bosworth it was the track team's fault that you didn't get your homework done," Ms. Okes finished for me.

"I didn't mean it that way, honest I didn't!"

"I know, Jo," Ms. Okes said quietly. "But that's how it was seen. Please make sure it doesn't happen anymore," she said.

I nodded and left Coach Okes' office as fast as I could. All the way home I thought about it. I'd let Mr. Bosworth think that track was my problem because I didn't want to tell him I forgot his assignment. But Ms. Okes got in trouble because of it.

Then I remembered Rod and our meeting at Antonio's. I'd let him think that Amy was me. Now Amy was barely speaking to me. I didn't know why she was so upset now. Saturday she had been really nice about it, trying to get me to tell Rod. But since then, she'd asked me if I'd told him, and after that she'd been pretty distant toward me. What a mess I'd made of things!

"Hi, Tails!" Jim came skidding up beside me on his bicycle. "Who was that guy I saw you with Saturday? Some new boyfriend?"

I looked at Jim's wide grin beneath his long nose and glasses and remembered I'd been pretty rude to him at Antonio's on Saturday. But I'd been so afraid he was going to call me Jo or say something to ruin everything. I shrugged. "Oh, he's a friend. We really just met on Saturday."

Jim's eyes narrowed a little, and he said, "A friend, but you just met on Saturday, huh? Sounds interesting. What do you know about him?"

"That's none of your business, Jim," I said, but I didn't want to be rude again.

"Aw, that's what I was afraid of. Here I am with your best interests at heart, and you don't even care. Is he nice? Will he treat you well? Does he have a car?"

"Stop it, Jim. It's not important. Besides, he spent most of the time looking at Amy, unfortunately."

"Aha, the truth comes out. You do care," Jim exclaimed. "Well, if it's any consolation, Jo, I didn't think either of them looked all that lovestruck about Amy. Which guy did you like, the one with the red hair?"

"Oh, go away, Jim. What do you know, anyway?"

"Hey, I go into Antonio's all the time. If I see them there, I'll put in a good word for you. After seeing you in the track meet the other day, I can tell them how well you run."

"Jim! Don't you dare!" I didn't think there was a chance Rod would be in Antonio's again soon, but if Jim did happen to see Rod somewhere, it could be a disaster.

Jim's eyebrows went up, and his mouth turned down in a mock hurt expression. "I was just trying to help, Tails."

"You're about as much help as an elephant in a glassware shop, Jim. If you meet him, do me a favor and just keep quiet, will you? And please quit calling me Tails."

"Sure, Tail—excuse me, Josephine!" he taunted. He pushed on the pedals of his bike and sped off down the street.

* * * * *

I told myself there was no reason to worry about Jim meeting Rod. But by Thursday of that week, Rod still hadn't called. I figured he didn't plan to meet any of us—ever again. I concentrated on track practice and on getting all my homework done on time.

I also called Amy a couple of times, but she was busy taking the twins to soccer practice one night. Another night, she just didn't want to talk. I hoped that in addition to ruining my chances with Rod, I hadn't also lost my best friend.

Finally, I went over to Amy's house one evening. It was so good to see her. I started apologizing the minute she came to the door. "Amy, I'm really sorry for the spot I put you in Saturday. Will you please forgive me?"

She opened the door and led me into the kitchen. "I'm not upset with you, Jo. I thought you knew that." She poured me a glass of milk and got out a bag of cookies.

"Well, then why—why haven't I seen you all week?" I asked. "Aren't you avoiding me?"

"Oh, no." She covered her mouth with her hand. "It's nothing like that, Jo. Come here. I'll show you." She led me into her room and closed the door. I sat down on the bed, and she put her finger to her lips for me to be quiet. Then she reached way back into her closet and brought out a bundle of white yarn. She spread it out across my lap. It was a gorgeous, soft white shawl. Or it would be when she finished crocheting it.

"It's beautiful!" I whispered.

"It's for my mother's birthday on Sunday," she said. "I just hope I get it done in time. I've been spending every spare minute on it, but it's been hard since I've been trying to keep it secret."

I felt much better when I left Amy's that night, even though she had given me another lecture about telling Rod the truth.

I felt awful that I'd met a terrific guy and would probably never see him again. I kept trying to figure out if Amy or I had said anything that might have made him think we were too childish or too crazy. Sometimes, I know I get carried away. But he didn't seem to be particularly bored with us. So why didn't he call?

Even the track meet Thursday wasn't a big deal. Duxberry's best runner had the flu, and they had a twelve-year-old entered in the 440. She was pretty good, for someone only about four feet ten. But it didn't feel all that great to beat her when she had to take three steps for every one of mine. Jim came to watch, but Amy had already told me she'd be at home working on her mother's present.

The one exciting thing I learned at the meet wasn't about track at all. Gretchen punched me and pointed out Mr. Bosworth in the stands. "Did you know he and Ms. Okes are getting married?" she asked me.

"No! Really? How do you know?" I couldn't believe it.

"Coach Okes told me one day when we were walking out together." Gretchen was bubbling with enthusiasm.

Wow, I thought. I was really happy for her. I wished I could be happy for me. I wanted the chance to get to know Rod. I'd really blown my chances with him, though.

But Thursday night when I was finishing my algebra, the phone rang. Mom called, "Jo? It's Rod Lingst for you." She gave me a special smile as I took the phone.

"Hi there!" he said cheerfully.

"Hi," I said, wondering if I could think of

78

anything to say. I could hardly hear because my heart was pounding against my rib cage as if I'd just finished three laps.

Rod told me he'd just finished a big project for English class. He said he had tests going on this week, and he'd been studying hard every night.

"So is that guard still tailing you? What's her name, Amy?" he asked.

"Pretty much," I said.

"Well, I wondered if you could shake yourself away from her Saturday afternoon so we could go bowling."

I was to the point of saying yes, when I realized that *I* was the person I was supposed to shake off, and he thought he was asking Amy. "Uh—no, I'm sorry. We have—um—Saturday—that is—my folks and I are going out of town this weekend. I really would like to see you, but—"

"That's okay. We'll find another time," he said. I could almost hear him smile over the phone. What a terrific voice he had.

We talked about movies and music. And because I said we were going out of town, he told me about traveling. His family had gone camping practically everywhere. One summer they'd spent a month at Yellowstone, and one year they'd gone to the Smoky Mountains. We were so busy talking, and Rod was so interesting when he described places, that I didn't even realize how much time had passed. Suddenly he said, "Yipes! Here I am rambling on, and it's getting late. I'll see you later, Jo."

"Bye," I said, feeling guilty about not telling him who he was *really* talking to.

"So, is he somebody you're interested in?" Mom asked. She came into the kitchen as I put down the receiver.

"Let's say I'd like to be interested in him."

"Well, when do we get to meet him?" she asked me.

"Oh—uh—not for a while," I said. "He's a freshman at West High, so he can't get over this way very often."

While I was talking to Mom, and even when I was trying to get to sleep, I kept thinking about Rod. How could I get him to like me—that is, me—and not Amy? How could I straighten out this mess without making him hate me?

Then suddenly I sat right up in bed. Why didn't he notice that my voice was different from Amy's? We don't sound alike at all. Amy's voice is high and soft. But my voice is deeper. So why hadn't Rod noticed? If he had, it would have solved my problem, I thought. But since he hadn't, what could I do now? How was I ever going to get out of this?

Ten

THE annual city-wide track and field day is probably the biggest thing on Coach Okes' calendar—except maybe this year when she's getting married. We hadn't heard about much else but the meet for weeks. She had us practicing and practicing every day after school. She posted last year's team scores and the winning scores down in the locker room. The Medbrook scores were nowhere near the winning scores. But this year, she said, would be different. It's true that some of us had bettered those times—not always—but occasionally at an after-school meet or in practice. I sure hoped we wouldn't disappoint Coach Okes. She was really looking forward to the meet.

On May eighteenth, I was still eating my breakfast and looking out the window at a pink sky when Coach Okes arrived. She was driving a borrowed van. I piled in along with the rest of the team for the ride to County Stadium. We all looked pretty sleepy—except for Coach Okes. She was humming.

All the teams in the city came to this meet. Middle school events were in the morning. Girls' track was first. The officials were still sipping coffee from styrofoam cups, and there was almost nobody in the stadium to watch us. The guys would have more spectators later in the morning, and the high school teams met in the afternoon. I supposed that way the crowd would get bigger through the day. But it meant that we were practically alone for our events.

Before each event, the competitors lined up facing the stands. The announcer introduced each person and school over the squeaky PA system. I thought all that attention would be a good idea later when there was someone to applaud. But first thing in the morning, the girls were embarrassed to be announced to empty seats. My parents said they'd come to watch me run, but even they hadn't shown up yet.

I sat on a bench rubbing my legs, watching and cheering as Jill bettered her best long-jump distance. She really looked good. And even though she only took third place, Coach Okes beamed. Then Gretchen lined up for the 100-yard dash. She took off at the sound of the gun as if she were the wind. We were all jumping and yelling for her. It didn't look like anyone could ever catch her. But suddenly, she crumpled up. She just bent over like a piece of tissue paper. Coach Okes was there in a second, helping her off the track. She had a cramp in her left leg, and she could hardly stretch the leg out.

We all thought we were pretty well warmed up. But after that, Coach had us doing all kinds of exercises along the sidelines. Nobody mentioned the relay. But I looked at Gretchen, white-faced and huddled in a blanket on the bench, and decided it would be a miracle if we got to run in it.

During the javelin throws, I sat down beside Gretchen. "How are you feeling?" I asked.

"Awful," she said. And she did look pretty miserable. Gretchen stretched her leg out in front of her. "I almost won it."

"Yeah, you were going great," I said. Then I looked at her expression and added, "You *will* win next time."

"Next year, you mean," she said, and her lip trembled. "By then I'll be in eighth grade, and eighth graders always win. I wanted to beat the eighth graders *this* year."

"It's okay, though," I told her. "It'll be all right. Next year you'll set a record."

She got up and limped around on her leg. "I don't know about the relay, Jo," she said.

"Don't worry," I told her. "It's not a big deal." But it was, and we both knew it. Of all the events, we had the best chance in the relay. Luckily, it would be a while before the relays began. I had no idea whether Gretchen would be all right or whether anybody else could run for her. I walked up and down a little, stretching out my legs.

Then it was my turn for the 440. I knew practically everyone who lined up for introductions. We stood in the sunlight while our names and schools were read, and I squinted up to see if Mom and Dad were there. They were, and just in front of them were Amy and Jim. Jim grinned and gave me a thumbs-up sign. Then, just as the announcer called my name and I stepped forward, I saw him. It was Rod Lingst. He was sitting three rows up, practically right in front of me! I couldn't believe it. He turned to someone and pointed toward us.

I wanted to disappear. I felt my face go red, and I bent my head to stare at the track. Did he see me? Sure he did, there was no way he wouldn't have. But what was I going to say to him now? How could I ever explain why the announcer called Jo Hartrum and the person who stepped out was me and not Amy?

And then I realized I was probably worrying for nothing. Why should I plan what I'd say when he'd probably never speak to me again anyway? Not now. Not after he knew I wasn't Amy . . . and that I'd lied to him. I felt cold, and the day seemed gray in spite of the sunlight.

We walked to our starting positions. Kathy Childs from Crestview was the best runner I'd seen or been up against. She was in the lane ahead of me, and she turned around to smile. It had been a long time since I'd run against her. I wondered if all those practices and all that work on pacing myself would make a difference. Then I thought about Rod and realized nothing made any difference to me. I was so ashamed of lying. And I liked Rod. I liked his letters and his sense of humor. And I'd ruined everything.

I heard the announcer. "On your marks." There wasn't anymore time. The gun went off, and automatically my legs responded. The white stripe of the lane flowed out in front, turned, and I followed it. The air was fresh and cool against my face. The early sun picked out bright patches of trees, billboards, and the stadium alongside the track. Everything seemed crisp. The whole world was edged with the clearness of the day. Even without my glasses I could see it. Everything was bright except me. And all I wanted to do was run away—away from the mess I'd created with Rod and the way I'd used Amy.

In a little while, everything inside me began to work, all moving together. My breath came in an easy rhythm. My arms and legs moved with it. Soon I couldn't think of Rod or anything else. There was just the pure joy of running, running as fast as I could, alive with the moment. I suddenly realized I was in the last turn, and Kathy was still way ahead of me. I stretched my legs, reaching farther and farther in front of me with every step. Everything in me reached and reached. The world blurred as I fixed my eyes on Kathy's shirt in front of me. Closer, closer . . . and then we crossed the finish.

My teammates were yelling along the sidelines when Kathy slowed and came over to shake hands with me.

"Nice race. Good job, Jo."

"You, too," I said. "Congratulations."

Kathy looked startled, then her face spread into a slow smile. "You know you're the one who won."

Then my team was all gathered around me yelling and slapping me on the back and pulling me off the field. "I did?" I could hardly believe what I was hearing.

In the midst of the excitement, I looked up into the stands. Mom and Dad were waving to me. Amy was cheering, and Jim gave a loud yell. But Rod was gone from his seat. I didn't see him anywhere.

Then there wasn't time to look for him anymore. The girls' events were running late, and the officials wanted to start the relays. I looked at Gretchen, then at Coach Okes. The coach shook her head. Jill and Lynn and I went over to sit with Gretchen to watch. She felt pretty awful.

"Hey, it's okay, you know?" Jill told her. "We'll do it next year."

"I doubt it," Gretchen said miserably. "We won't have Jo next year. She's going to high school."

For a minute I felt a twinge of sadness that I wouldn't be on the team.

"We'll miss you all right, Jo, especially those long legs," Lynn said. "But Gretchen, don't you worry. I plan to grow."

We all looked at her. Lynn's the shortest of us all, and she'd told us she stopped growing when she was ten. Suddenly, Gretchen smiled. Then she started to giggle. Pretty soon we were all laughing hysterically.

We heard the gun go off. It was a tough contest, especially between the Crestview and Hudson teams. Hudson was ahead at the last lap. But Kathy Childs was taller than the Hudson girl, and she really flew the last stretch. It was beautiful to watch her. When she crossed the finish, I was shouting and jumping as much as if she'd been on our team instead of Crestview's.

"You'd have beat her, Jo," Gretchen said softly.

I shook my head. "Hard to tell. She's awfully good."

The next minute, though, I felt differently toward Kathy Childs. I suddenly noticed Rod standing at the sidelines. Kathy came running off the track. She threw her arms around Rod and gave him a big kiss on the cheek. Rod hugged her and grinned broadly. I felt a big chill. If I could, I'd have gotten out of there. But there was no place to go. Besides, all my team would wonder what had gotten into me. So I just sat there, feeling miserable. Long after they had walked away arm in arm, I could still see Kathy standing there kissing Rod.

I couldn't help but remember that he'd asked me for a date a couple of weekends ago, and I'd turned him down. But he was still calling me and writing me letters. It was hard to believe Rod was the type to have girls in every school.

The officials hurried the awards ceremony, because we were behind schedule. When it was my turn to go up, I barely got my trophy before they were calling Kathy's relay team. They were walking up as I walked away. I hurried off the field, looking down.

Suddenly, I realized someone was standing in front of me. I glanced up and looked straight into Rod's dark eyes.

"Oh!" I said. Score one for my brilliant conversational ability.

"Hi, Jo. Congratulations!" Rod was smiling. At me!

"Um—thank you," I said. "Uh, listen, Rod, I—uh—" Then it registered. He was calling me by my right name! I stopped. I didn't know what to say. He just grinned and lifted one eyebrow.

"I'm sorry about the picture," I blurted out.

He laughed. "It's all right, Jo. Jim wanted me to keep the joke going a little longer, but then Jim never did know when to stop a joke. When I saw you here today, I decided—"

"What joke? Jim who?" I demanded.

"Jim Santo, of course," Rod grinned. "Oh, I guess I forgot to tell you. Jim and I have been friends for years. We go to the same church.

That's how I knew all about you."

"Huh?" I was thoroughly confused by now.

Then it got worse. Kathy Childs came up waving her relay trophy. "Rod! Look at what I got!" She threw her empty arm around him and gave him a big hug.

Rod smiled and hugged her back. I felt awful standing there. Then he said, "See, I told you you could do it. Jo, I want you to meet Kathy."

"We've met," I said and tried to smile. All the while, I was telling myself that I should have known. Anybody as good-looking as Rod wouldn't be interested in me.

"Have you shown Mom and Dad?" Rod was asking Kathy.

"Not yet," she said. "See you later, Jo. Tell your teammates I'm really sorry you guys couldn't compete."

"I will," I said automatically.

"C'mon, Jo. I have to talk to you." He smiled at me, and I realized I was tilting my head up to look at him. It was a new position for me. Usually, I look down on everything. I decided I liked it.

"I don't understand," I said as Rod led me to a seat in the stands.

"Kathy's my stepsister. We have a bet going. Now that she's won the relay I have to win my race this afternoon, or I owe her a pizza."

"Oh, your sister!" I said. And that's when I noticed that the sun was shining, birds were singing, and I felt terrific. "But how did you know who I was?" I asked.

"Well, when I got the balloon with the card on it, I thought you must be a fun person. I knew Jim went to your school, so I asked him if he knew you."

Rod smiled, and something in the way he was looking at me made me want to grin. A delicious shiver went down my spine. "And?" I asked.

"He really laughed when I told him about your card. He said you lived right down the street and you'd been friends forever. He also said you were really nice. And then he gave me your picture."

"What?" Suddenly I remembered that day we got our school pictures and Jim asked me to trade. I'd forgotten all about it.

"So when I got the letter with the other picture, Jim told me it was your friend. He thought it was a great joke. He even wanted me to keep it up longer. But—"

I looked at him. I didn't know whether to be mad or glad that it was finally over.

"I'd have known you anyway at Antonio's. Your friend's voice isn't anything like yours. But we were waiting to see what you would say and how you would handle it."

Rod's eyes twinkled with mischief for a minute. Then he got serious—well, at least a little serious. "Jo, I'm tired of only talking to you by phone and letter. I figured that until we got this mix-up straightened out you'd keep turning me down every time I tried to get us together. And I'd like to get to know you in person."

I nodded. "I'd like that, too."

I glanced up in the stands. Amy was still sitting with Jim. They both had huge smiles. And this time I got a thumbs-up sign from both of them. I looked back at Rod.

"The thing I didn't know," Rod said, "was that you were a runner. I was really surprised to see you this morning." He nodded his head. "This is great! We both run. We can explore all the running trails in the city this summer."

I loved the sound of it. I loved the way he was looking at me. It was just the way I'd pictured it. And I loved the way he was making plans for us to see more of each other. I felt like I was ten feet tall, and for once I didn't mind a bit.

About the Author

VICTORIA M. ALTHOFF likes to write about heroes, both male and female. She wrote her first story in second grade. She remembers that it was fifteen pages of double-ruled handwriting practice paper. And the hero of that story is now her husband.

Where does she get her ideas? Vicki says that ideas for books are everywhere. "I was watching a balloon launch one day and wondered what would happen if somebody really interesting found the balloon, and a special friendship developed out of it."

When she's not writing fiction, Vicki is a production editor for school textbooks. She has also been a newspaper reporter, a city planner, and a technical writer and editor.

Vicki likes to take walks on the trails of a wooded park near her home in Columbus, Ohio. She and her family enjoy traveling in the United States, and they recently visited Germany. Vicki also enjoys music and reading. Her favorite books include mysteries, adventures, and, of course, romances.